Mommy's Gone to

Denise D. Crosson, Ph.D. • Illustrat

CRP

CENTRAL RECOVERY PRESS

LAS VEGAS, NEVADA

One morning, Janey woke up to a beautiful sunshiny day. How strange, she thought as she looked around the room, Mommy usually comes to wake me up. She picked up her favorite doll and off they went to look for Mommy.

They looked in Mommy's bedroom, but it was quiet and dark.

They looked in Mommy's bathroom, but Mommy wasn't there.

They looked in Mommy's office, but it was empty too. Where could Mommy be?

Janey heard a sound in the kitchen. Could that be Mommy? She skipped down the stairs and found Daddy making breakfast and packing her lunch. How strange, Janey thought, Mommy does that every morning.

"Where's Mommy?" Janey asked her Daddy.

Daddy said, "Janey, sit down and start your breakfast. We can talk about Mommy in a minute."

Daddy sat down next to Janey and said, "Janey, some things are hard
for daddies to talk about, and this is one of them. Before I tell you,
I hope you know Mommy and I love you very much."
Janey nodded, but she was scared. She didn't know what to think.

Daddy hugged Janey and said, "Mommy is sick and has gone to the hospital
to get better. She'll be gone until the doctor says she can come home.
Your Grandmom is coming to help us out while Mommy is away."
Janey didn't know what to think. This is not what she expected Daddy to say!

Janey started to cry. "I want my Mommy. Why has Mommy gone?"
Daddy stroked Janey's hair and said, "I know you want your Mommy;
I want Mommy too. If she could, Mommy would be here with us,
but right now she is too sick." Janey looked up at her Daddy.
"I saw Mommy last night, and she didn't look sick to me!"

Daddy smiled at Janey. "I know. It's hard to see where Mommy's sick.
Do you remember how sometimes Mommy would go to sleep and you
couldn't wake her up? And how sometimes she was really angry with you,
even though you didn't do anything wrong?" Janey nodded.
"Well, those were all signs that she was sick.
Your Mommy has a disease called addiction. We just didn't realize it before.
Now, she's gone away to learn how to get better."

Janey kept crying. "She will come home, right?" Daddy chuckled.
"Of course she'll come home, and next week we'll even go visit her in the hospital."
Janey was glad. She didn't want her Mommy to be sick or to be gone.
But she was happy Mommy had gone to get better because
she didn't like when Mommy did those things.

"Will we get ice cream when we visit Mommy?" Janey sounded hopeful.
"Ice cream?" Daddy asked.
"When I was in the hospital, I got to eat all the ice cream I wanted," Janey said, smiling.

"Oh, I forgot you were in the hospital when you had your tonsils taken out. Well, Mommy is sick in a different way, so she's in a different hospital. She's in a hospital called a treatment center. If they don't have ice cream at Mommy's hospital, we'll get some on the way home. Okay?"

Now Janey's smile was bigger.
Daddy finished packing Janey's lunch and drove her to school.

When Janey got out of school, her Grandmom was there to pick her up.
They went to the park on the way home. Janey noticed Grandmom was not
very happy. Janey was scared. Maybe Mommy was sicker than Daddy said!
She was afraid to ask Grandmom, so she tried to play.

After Janey and Grandmom got home from the park, Daddy came home from work.
Janey ran to him crying, "Is Mommy okay? What's wrong with her?"
Daddy said, "Mommy's better. In fact, she's better than she's been in awhile."
"Then why can't she come home now?" Janey demanded.

"Mommy's better, but she's not ready to come home yet.
The doctors are teaching her how to be healthy," Daddy said.

Janey wondered if it was her fault that Mommy got sick.
"Of course not," Daddy said. "Remember when you had your tonsils taken out?"
Janey nodded. "Well, that wasn't your fault, right?
And Mommy's sickness isn't anyone's fault either."

Janey felt better knowing that she didn't make Mommy sick.

Janey missed Mommy every morning when she woke up on her own.
But every day when she went down to breakfast, she saw Daddy and Grandmom.
Janey felt less lonely listening to them talk.

One morning when Janey woke up, Daddy said "Today is the day we go see Mommy! It'll be a lo-o-o-o-ng car ride." Janey didn't like long car rides, but she was so excited to see Mommy that she didn't complain.

The car ride turned out to be fun. Daddy and Grandmom played car games with her, and the ride was one she had never been on before. Janey saw farms and factories. Big towns and small towns. Spotted cows and brown horses and playful gray squirrels. There were so many new things to see that Janey could hardly believe how quickly they got to the treatment center.

While Daddy parked the car, Janey looked around.
"This doesn't look at all like the hospital I was in when I was sick," Janey thought.
"This building is not big or tall and there are no ambulances coming and going."

When they got to the door, a nice lady let them in.
Daddy and Grandmom signed papers. Janey asked, "Do I have to sign papers, too?"
The nice lady smiled and gave Janey a pen and paper and said, "Why don't you
draw your Mommy a picture and sign it while I go get her."
Janey was happy the lady was nice to her,
but happier that she'd finally get to see Mommy.

When the lady left to go get Mommy, Janey thought,
"The people at my hospital were nice, but not this nice. No wonder Mommy wants
to be here if the people are always so nice. Maybe she'll never want to come home."

Finally the lady came back with Janey's Mommy.
Janey ran and hugged Mommy tightly.
"I missed you so much. When are you coming home?"

Mommy smiled at Janey and said, "I missed you so much too,
and I'm very glad you are here. I'm not sure yet when I'll be coming home.
I need to be here until the doctor thinks I can stay healthy on my own."

Janey looked at Mommy. She looked at her face, her arms, her legs, and her body.
Janey couldn't see anything wrong. Mommy looked just fine.
"You look okay to me. I can't see where you're sick. Where are you sick, Mommy?"

Mommy didn't answer right away. Janey thought Mommy might cry.
Finally, Mommy said, "Janey, I'm sick inside where you can't see.
That's why it took Daddy and me so long to realize I needed help.
The good news is I'm getting lots of help here. I'm learning things I need to do
so I can stay healthy when I come home."

Daddy, Grandmom, and Mommy talked while Janey drew pictures and watched the other people. Some of them looked really different from Mommy. Some were older, some were younger; some were men, and some had different skin colors; but they all looked very happy to see their families.

As Daddy, Grandmom, and Janey were getting ready to leave, Janey asked, "How did you know you were sick if it's only on the inside?"

Mommy sat down and looked at Janey. "Being a good Mommy to you
and a good wife to Daddy are two of the most important things in the world to me,"
she said. "I was too sick to take care of anyone. I was grumpy with you and Daddy
when I shouldn't have been, and sometimes I scared you. I even wrecked the car!
That scared me. We finally realized I needed help."

Janey liked that Mommy answered her questions even if Janey didn't completely understand the answers. Janey didn't know why, but now she felt big and brave. So she said, "Mommy, you look tired. You should take a nap."

Mommy laughed and gave Janey a great big hug.
This was the best Janey had felt since Mommy went to the hospital.
Janey waved good-bye as she and Daddy and Grandmom walked to the car.

"When can we see Mommy again?" Janey asked as she got into the car. "We'll come back next week and every week until Mommy comes home," Daddy said. Janey still missed Mommy, but she was glad that Mommy was getting better. She fell asleep thinking how happy she would be when Mommy came home all better.

When she woke up, Daddy was carrying her into the house and it was already dark.
Daddy tucked Janey into her bed and said, "I love you. Sleep tight."
As she fell back asleep, Janey hugged her favorite doll. She remembered how
good it was to see Mommy and hear her laugh today. Janey still missed Mommy,
but she knew now that Mommy was getting better and would soon be home.

The End

Talking with Children about Addiction Treatment
A Guide for Parents

1. **Focus on the positive.** Anytime it's necessary to explain a difficult situation to a child, such as when a parent starts addiction treatment, try to balance happy times with times not so happy. Even if these are simple things, it helps teach that in the best of times there are things that are not perfect and in difficult times there are things worth celebrating.

2. **Keep it simple—at a child's level.** When talking with more than one child, speak at the youngest level. Once everyone understands the basics, encourage questions. If there is a large age difference, talk to everyone first and then follow up individually.

3. **Be completely honest.** Start with something like, "Mommy's gone to the hospital to get help for her drug use." Watch and listen to the child's response and answer any questions.

4. **Initiate the conversation;** do not wait for the child to ask about where the parent is or what has and will be happening. Putting off this important discussion only increases the child's sense of uncertainty and worry.

5. **Do not lecture.** Do not talk at or down to the child. Don't assume this is too complex a topic for children. Don't tell the child about what he or she should feel or believe. Ask about feelings, and then listen carefully to the answers. You want to present a calm presence so the child will feel safe to share whatever emotions he or she is experiencing.

6. **Be helpful; try to understand the concerns, feelings, and beliefs of the child.** Once you understand, offer explicit help and support. This might sound like, "You've told me you are feeling _____. When I feel _____ it helps me if the people I love do _____. Would that be something you'd like? Is there something you can tell me to do that would work better for you?" Remember, all children need reassurance. Younger children often only need basic information and consistent reassurance that they are not to blame and that the absent parent loves them and will be back.

7. **Share your own feelings and concerns.** It's important to give a simple honest disclosure of your emotional state, but it should be framed positively and reassuringly. For example: "With Daddy gone for several weeks, I sometimes feel sad. Fortunately, Grandma is helping us out and that makes things easier for me. All of your help has really meant a lot to me, too. I'm sorry if I was grumpy this morning. I don't want to take out feeling sad on you." Remember to not make the child your confidant.

8. **Share your values,** including that people we love are loveable even when they disappoint or inconvenience us. Communicate that addiction and mental illness are diseases like diabetes and high blood pressure that need treatment and support.

9. **Be available;** do not make the "crisis" the entire focus of your lives. While you may need to eliminate some family activities, keep those important for your own self-care and support. You cannot support others or your children without first taking care of your own needs.

10. **Be patient and supportive.** It is common for children under stress to be extra needy and fall back on behavior they grew out of months before. If the behavior goes on too long or seems beyond your ability, please talk with your child's primary health care provider. It may be a good idea to ask a family member or friend of the same sex as the absent parent to spend extra time with the child.

11. **Be clear and specific about everything,** including that you are available and want your children to talk about feelings, questions, or worries at any time. It is important you are consistent and reassuring. If you are overwhelmed and worried, settle yourself and get the support you need before starting the conversation with your child.

Important Talking Points to Remember

Neither the child nor others in
the family caused the problem.

* * *

Neither the child nor others in the
family are able to cure the disease,
but effective treatment is available
and the parent / family member
is receiving treatment.

* * *

Neither the child nor others in
the family can control the disease.

The most important thing
the child and other family
members can do is take
good care of themselves.

* * *

Taking good care of ourselves
always includes communicating
feelings, making healthy choices
that help us, and celebrating who
we are—specifically our strengths
and abilities—as individuals
and as a family.

ABOUT THE AUTHOR

Denise D. Crosson, Ph.D. has been a nurse for twenty-five years, a nurse practitioner for nine years, and a nurse researcher for five years. Her first job working with children was in high school as a lifeguard and swim instructor at the YMCA. Throughout her nursing career Crosson has worked with children and their families in hospital, home, hospice, and community-based settings. She earned a masters and doctoral degree from Virginia Commonwealth University where she was a fellow in the VA-LEND neurodevelopmental disabilities training program, which focused on children and families. Her dissertation research focused on short- and long-term effects of preterm birth on childhood development.

Crosson lives in Las Vegas, Nevada. This is her first book for children.

ABOUT THE ILLUSTRATOR

Mike Motz is an award-winning illustrator from Canada who has illustrated twenty-five children's books. His website, www.mikemotz.com, boasts a team of some of the most talented illustrators working in children's literature.

CENTRAL RECOVERY PRESS

Central Recovery Press (CRP) is committed to publishing exceptional material addressing addiction treatment and recovery, including original and quality books, audio/visual communications, and web-based new media. Through a diverse selection of titles, it seeks to impact the behavioral healthcare field with a broad range of unique resources for professionals, recovering individuals, and their families. For more information, visit www.centralrecoverypress.com.

CRP donates a portion of its proceeds to *The Foundation for Recovery,* a non-profit organization local and national in scope. Its purpose is to promote recovery from addiction through a variety of forums, such as direct services, research and development, education, study of recovery alternatives, public awareness, and advocacy.

Central Recovery Press, Las Vegas, 89129
© 2008 by Central Recovery Press, Las Vegas, NV

ISBN-13: 978-0-9799869-1-8
ISBN-10: 0-9799869-1-5

All rights reserved. Published 2008. Printed in the United States of America.
No part of this publication may be reproduced, stored in a retrieval system,
or transmitted in any form or by any means, electronic, mechanical, photocopying,
recording, or otherwise, without the written permission of the publisher.
15 14 13 12 11 10 09 08   1 2 3 4 5

Publisher: Central Recovery Press
          3371 N Buffalo Drive
          Las Vegas, NV 89129

Edited by Nancy A. Schenck and Laura VanDeusen
Typeset by Sara Streifel, Think Creative Design

CENTRAL RECOVERY PRESS
LAS VEGAS, NEVADA